This book should be returned to any branch of the
Lancashire County Library on or before the date shown

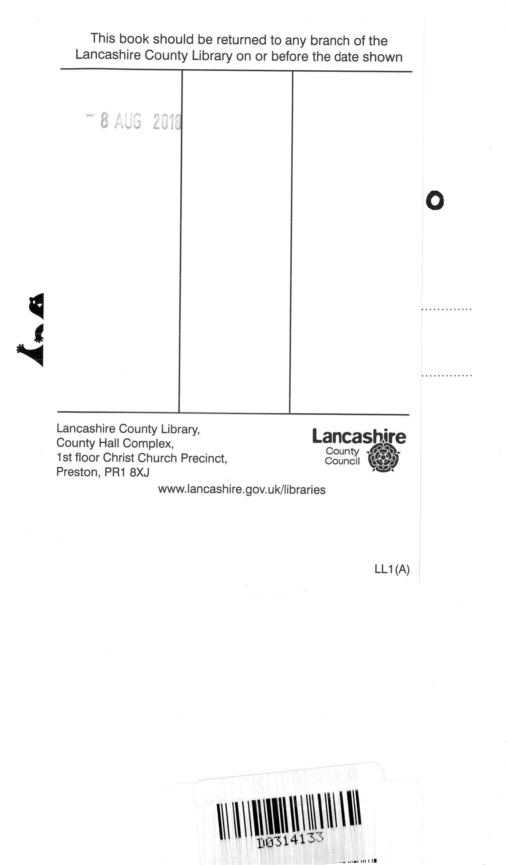

- 8 AUG 2018

Lancashire County Library,
County Hall Complex,
1st floor Christ Church Precinct,
Preston, PR1 8XJ

**Lancashire**
County
Council

www.lancashire.gov.uk/libraries

LL1(A)

For Phillip - the best daddy -
and for my very special Amelia - DH
For Charlie - CT

First published in Great Britain and in the USA in 2017 by
Otter-Barry Books, Little Orchard, Burley Gate, Hereford, HR1 3QS

This paperback edition first published in Great Britain in 2018

A catalogue record for this book is available from the British Library.

ISBN 978-1-910959-92-3

Illustrated with mixed media and collage

Printed in China

1 3 5 7 9 8 6 4 2

# My Daddy is a Silly Monkey

Story by Dianne Hofmeyr
Pictures by Carol Thompson

Otter-Barry BOOKS

My daddy is a great **BIG** bear.

He gets out of bed and

grizzles and grouches and scratches

and yawns.

My daddy is...

a naughty **Crocodile.**

He gives a **toothy grin**

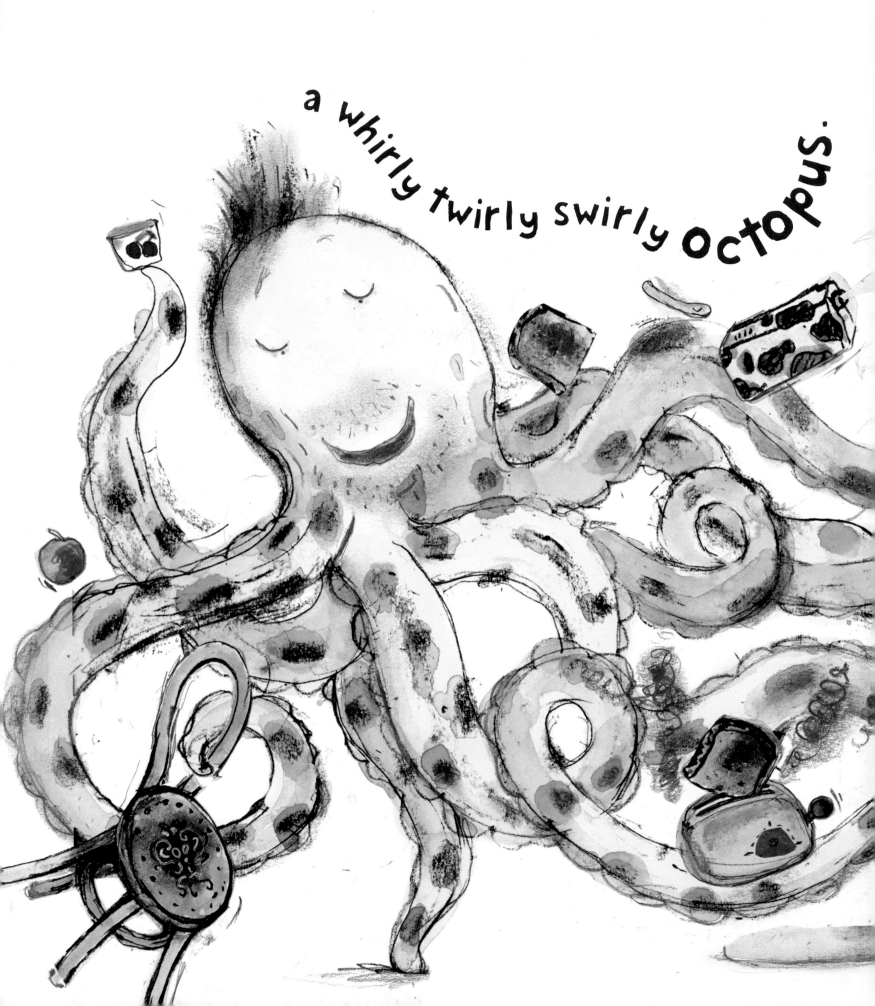

a whirly twirly swirly octopus.

He brushes my hair,

sends a text,

topples a chair,

spills the milk,

burns the toast,

ties my laces

and juggles my lunch.

My daddy is...

a SILLY monkey.

He chitters and CHATTERS and monkeys about,

and makes me very, VERY late for school.

My daddy is...

a **humungous** whale.

After school he splashes and wallows and spouts and swallows.

My daddy is...

He hippity hops,

flips and flops

and flies as high as the moon.

My daddy is...

a ravenous TIGER.

He mixes and mashes and gnashes his dinner until his tummy is **SO** full.

But not quite full enough!

**Because then he is...**

a gallumping, growling

monster!

**"Eat your dinner!"**

**"Tidy up!"**

**"Get into the bath!"**

**"Brush your teeth!"**

**"Or...**

Aaarhh!

And...

catch you!

At the end of the day my daddy is too tired to play.

He's not a bear,

not a crocodile,

not an octopus,

not a whale.

He's not
a kangaroo,

or a tiger,

or a monster.

He's not even a silly monkey.

He is...

just my lovely

**daddy**.

"Good night, Daddy."

"Good night, Sweetheart."

# About the Author and Illustrator

**Dianne Hofmeyr** grew up on the tip of southern Africa. Her acclaimed picture books include *The Magic Bojabi Tree* (with Piet Grobler), which was nominated for the 2014 Kate Greenaway Award and *Zeraffa Giraffa* (with Jane Ray), which is on The Sunday Times' Top 100 Children's Classics list. She lives in west London.
www.diannehofmeyr.com

• • •

**Carol Thompson** has written and illustrated more than 60 books for children and her work has been translated into over 20 languages. She is an IBBY UK committee member. She lives in Leicestershire.
www.instagram.com/carolthompson41/